To my friend Pamela.
M.N.

To the memory of Lilly and John,
and also to Benny and Floyd,
two large, furry, cake-eating cats.
S.W.

LITTLE TIGER PRESS
An imprint of Magi Publications
1 The Coda Centre, 189 Munster Road, London SW6 6AW
www.littletigerpress.com
First published in Great Britain 2002

ISBN 1 85430 797 5

A CIP catalogue record for this book is
available from the British Library

Printed in Belgium by Proost
2 4 6 8 10 9 7 5 3 1

Boswell
the kitchen cat

Marjorie Newman
illustrated by Suzanne Watts

LITTLE TIGER PRESS
London

Boswell the kitchen cat loved to cook.

Sizzling sausages,
luscious lasagne,
perfect pies.

Scrumptious!

But Boswell didn't like mess, and he really didn't like cleaning!

Sweeping the floor, scrubbing the cooker, washing the dishes.

It was very hard work and very, very boring!

Lizzie the kitchen mouse
and her family loved
messy kitchens.

Syrupy slops,
toasty titbits,
cheesy crumbs.

But they never found a single scrap
in Boswell's kitchen! And they were
always very, very hungry!!!

Until, that is, one day . . .

Boswell was
having a party.
He'd invited all of his
friends, and he set
about cooking an
enormous feast!

All day long
he mixed
and stirred . . .

he greased and baked.

He made a
tremendous
mess!

He was enjoying
himself so much
that he didn't
notice the **time!**

DING! DONG!

"Yikes!" cried Boswell, "they've arrived!" He looked around at all the mess, but it was just too late. The cleaning would have to wait!

And so the party began. Fabulous flans,
delicious doughnuts, lip-smacking lollipops...

all washed down with lashings of orangeade.
Boswell and his friends ate … and ate … and ate!

Meanwhile, back in the kitchen, the mice couldn't believe their luck.

"All this mess will feed us for a week!" squeaked Lizzie.

The mice hurried around here and there, collecting nibbles and titbits.

They started to sneak it past the partying cats when . . .

"Mice!" cried Boswell, staggering into his kitchen.

"Cat!" cried Lizzie, staggering into Boswell!
"Please don't eat us!" she sobbed.

"Eat you!" he said. "I couldn't eat another thing!
Well, perhaps just one tiny little mouse."

But luckily for the mice Boswell happened
to look around . . .

AAAH!

and found a sparkling clean kitchen!

The floor was swept,
the cooker was gleaming,
and the dishes were squeaky clean.
There wasn't a scrap of
mess anywhere!

Boswell suddenly had a very good idea!

From that day on Boswell still mixed
and stirred and cooked and baked.

He still made a truly dreadful mess,
but he didn't care one bit, because . . .

every evening Lizzie and her family
came and gobbled up all the mess!

And as a special treat,
each Friday . . .

Boswell baked a great big cheddar cheese pie!
And they all ate happily ever after.